Our World, Our Home

# Over on a Desert

## Count the baby animals that live in the driest places

By Marianne Berkes Illustrated by Jill Dubin

Over on a desert,
resting in the hot sun,
lived a tall mother camel
and her little calf **one**.

"Kneel," said the mother.
"I kneel," said the **one**.
So they knelt in the desert,
resting in the hot sun.

ASIA

Arabian Desert

1

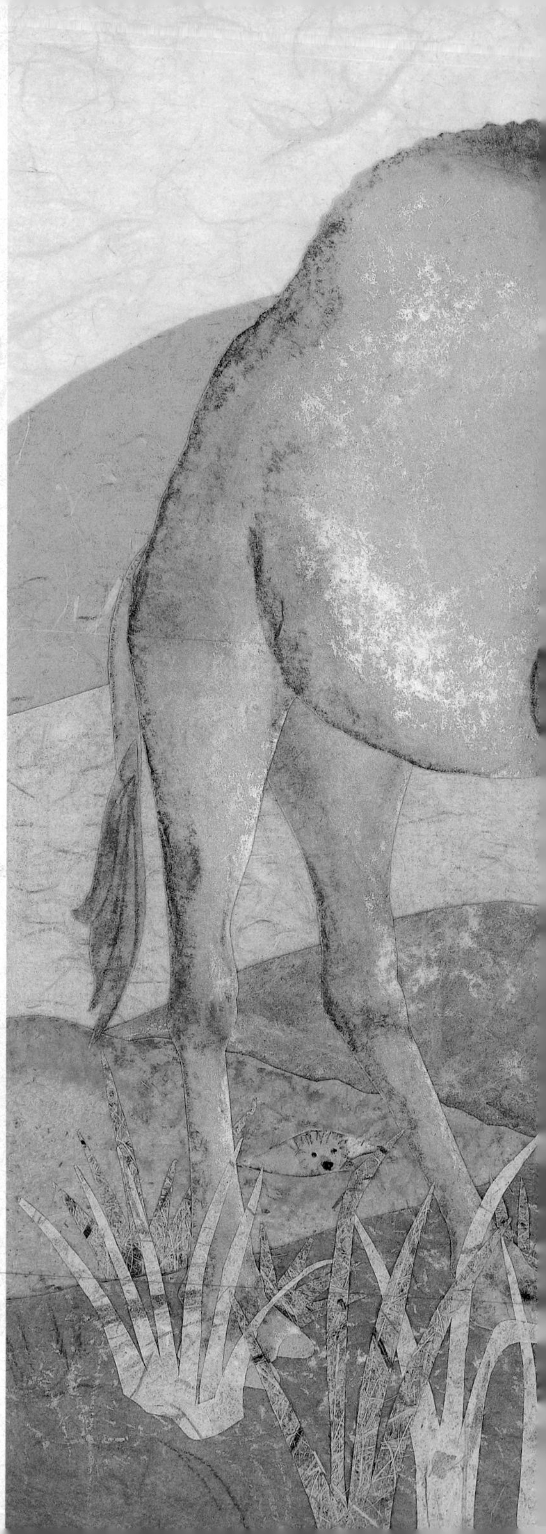

Over on a desert,
where the barrel cactus grew,
lived a mother gila monster
and her little hatchlings **two**.

“Flick,” said the mother.
“We flick,” said the **two**.
So they flicked with their tongues,
where the barrel cactus grew.

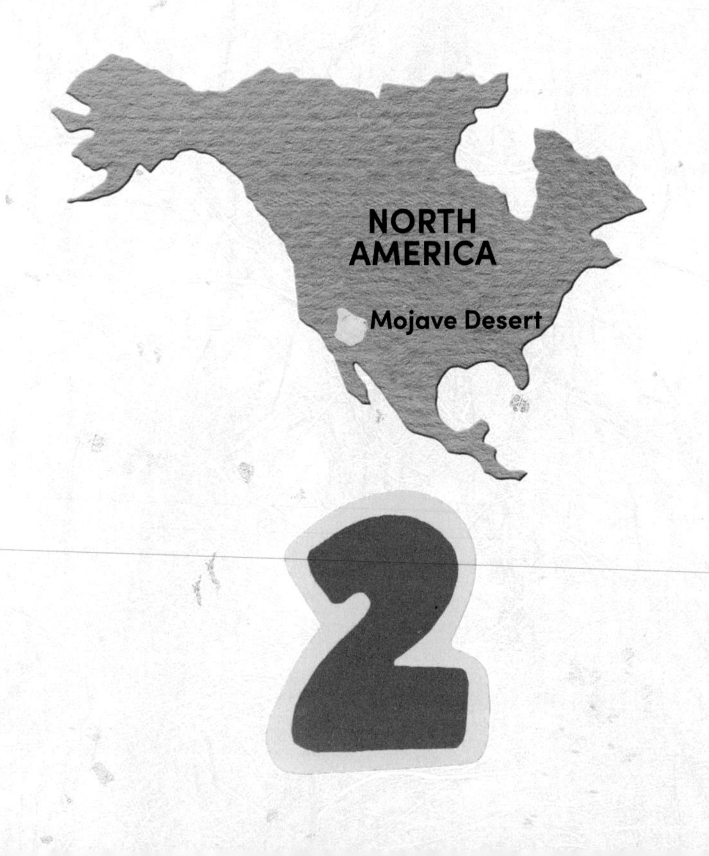


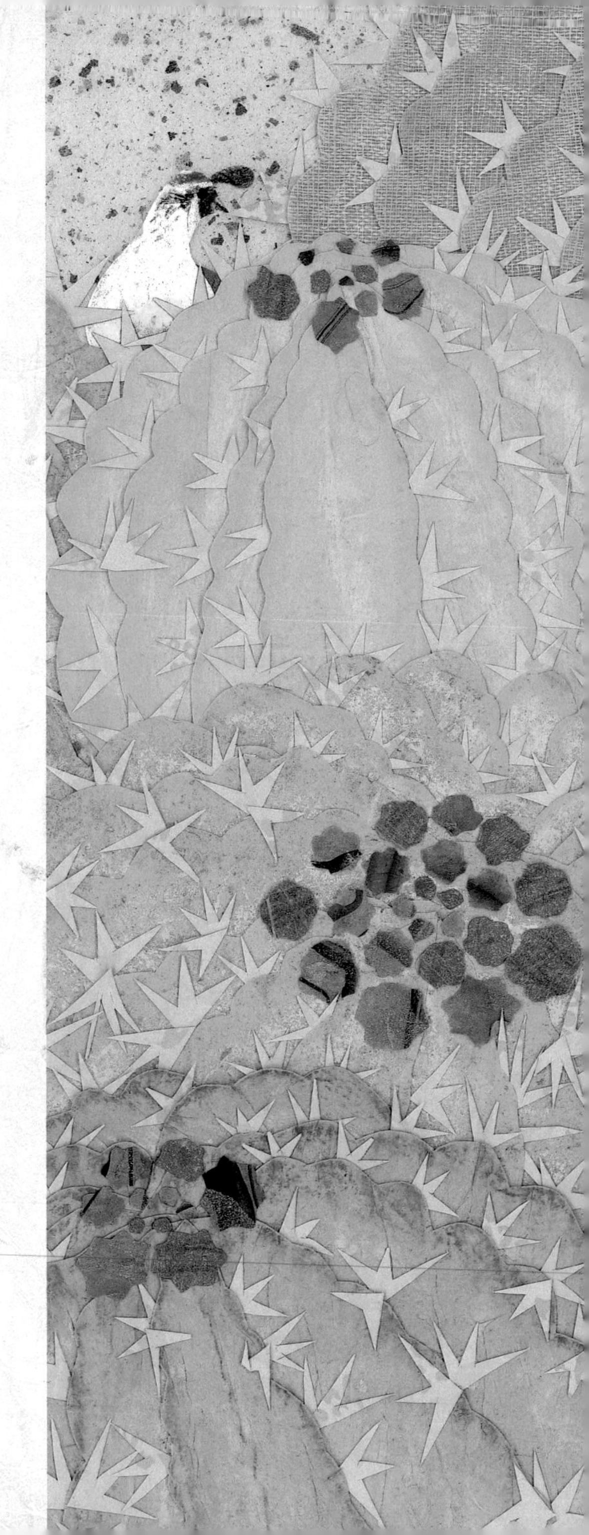

Over on a desert,
near a camelthorn tree,
lived a slender mother meerkat
and her little pups **three**.

"Stand" said the mother
"We stand," said the **three**.
So they stood and they watched
near a camelthorn tree.

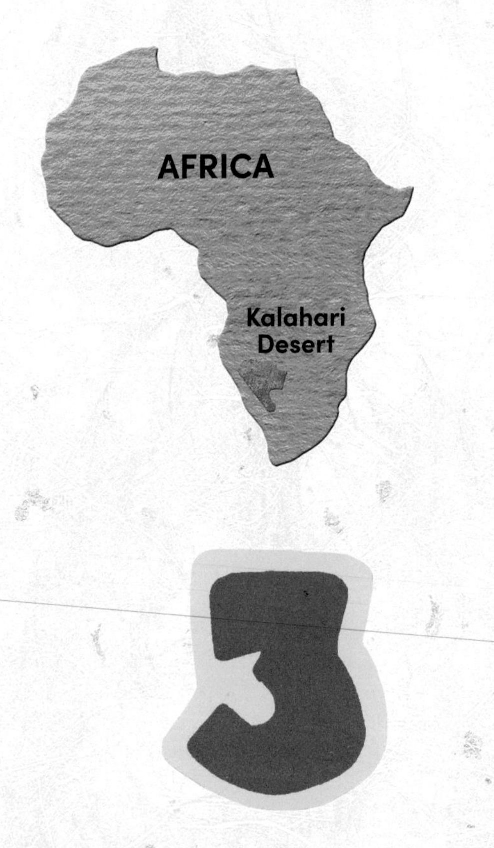

Over on a desert,
on a hot, sandy floor,
lived a wild mother dingo
and her little pups **four**.

"Sniff," said the mother.
"We sniff," said the **four**.
So they sniffed in a pack
on a hot, sandy floor.

Great Sandy Desert
AUSTRALIA

4

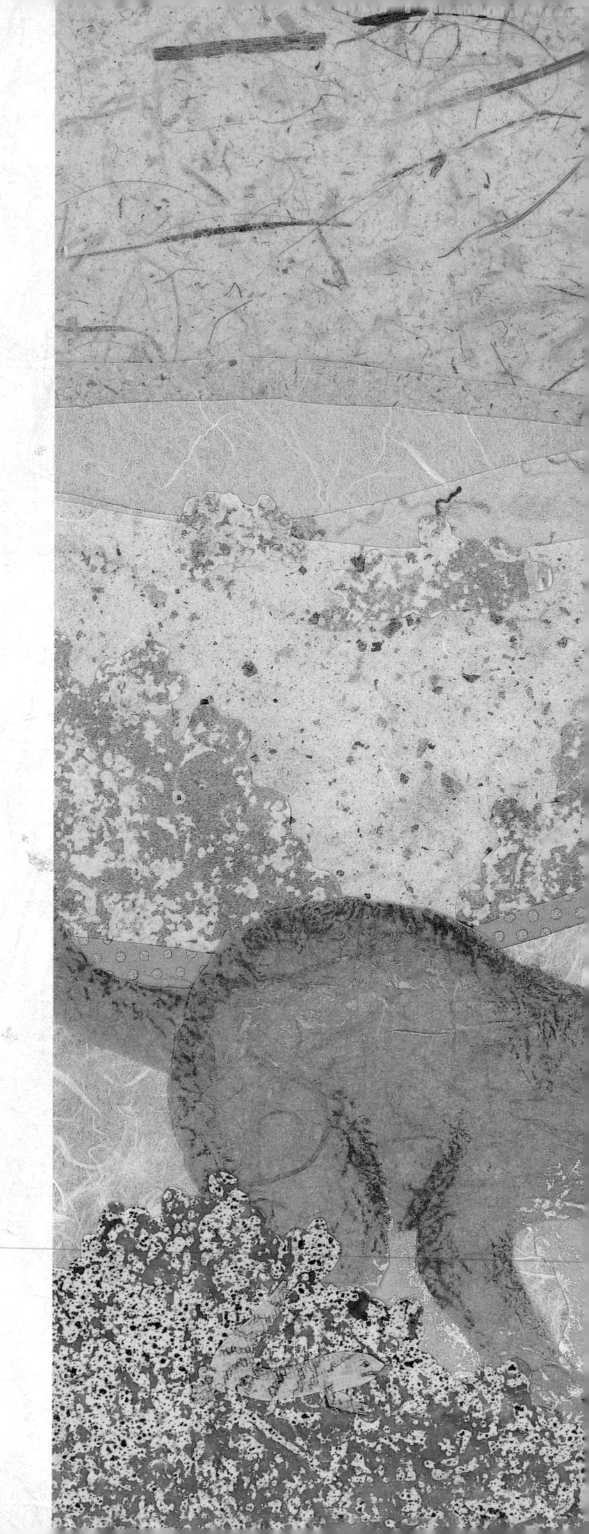

Over on a desert,
where mesquite trees thrive,
lived a mother armadillo
and her little pups **five**.

"Dig," said the mother.
"We dig," said the **five**.
So they dug with their claws
where mesquite trees thrive.

Over on a desert,
eating cactus that pricks,
lived a mother javelina
and her little reds **six**.

“Snort,” said the mother.
“We snort,” said the **six**.
So they grunted and they snorted,
eating cactus that pricks.

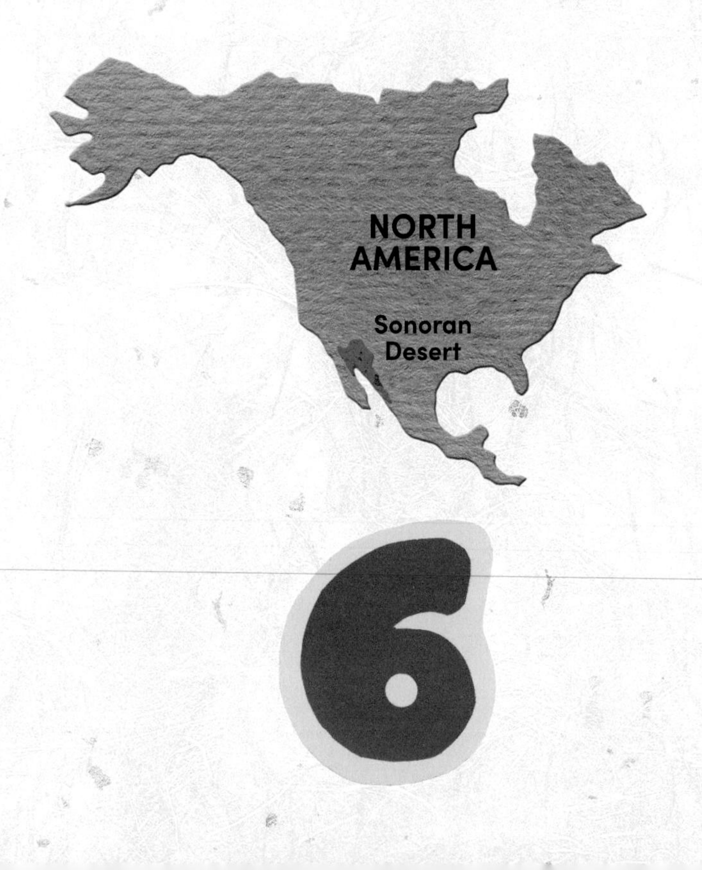

Over on a desert,
where saguaros reach the heavens,
lived a mother desert tortoise
and her little hatchlings **seven**.

"Hide," said the mother.
"We hide," said the **seven**.
So they hid in their shells,
where saguaros reach the heavens.

Over on a desert,
where they often go out late,
lived a shy mother jerboa
and her little pups **eight**.

"Jump," said the mother.
"We jump," said the **eight**.
So they jumped way up high
where they often go out late.

ASIA

Gobi Desert

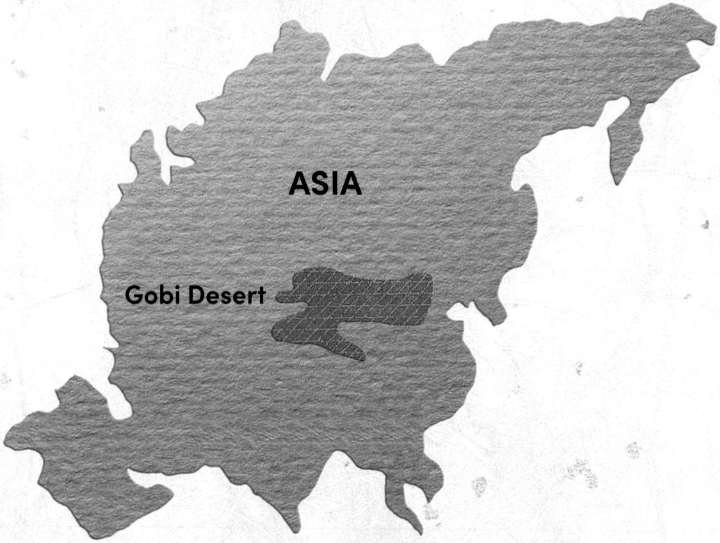

8

Over on a desert,
in the hot sunshine,
lived a mother roadrunner
and her little chicks **nine.**

"Coo," said the mother.
"We coo," said the **nine**.
So they cooed as they ran
in the hot sunshine.

Over on a desert,
in their underground den,
lived a clever fennec fox
and his little kits **ten**.

"Listen," said the father.
"We listen," said the **ten**,
as they heard the sound of laughing
from their underground den.

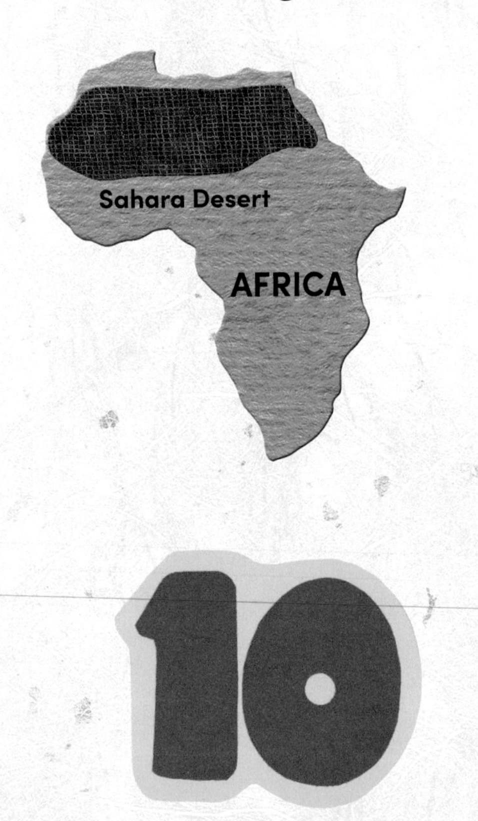

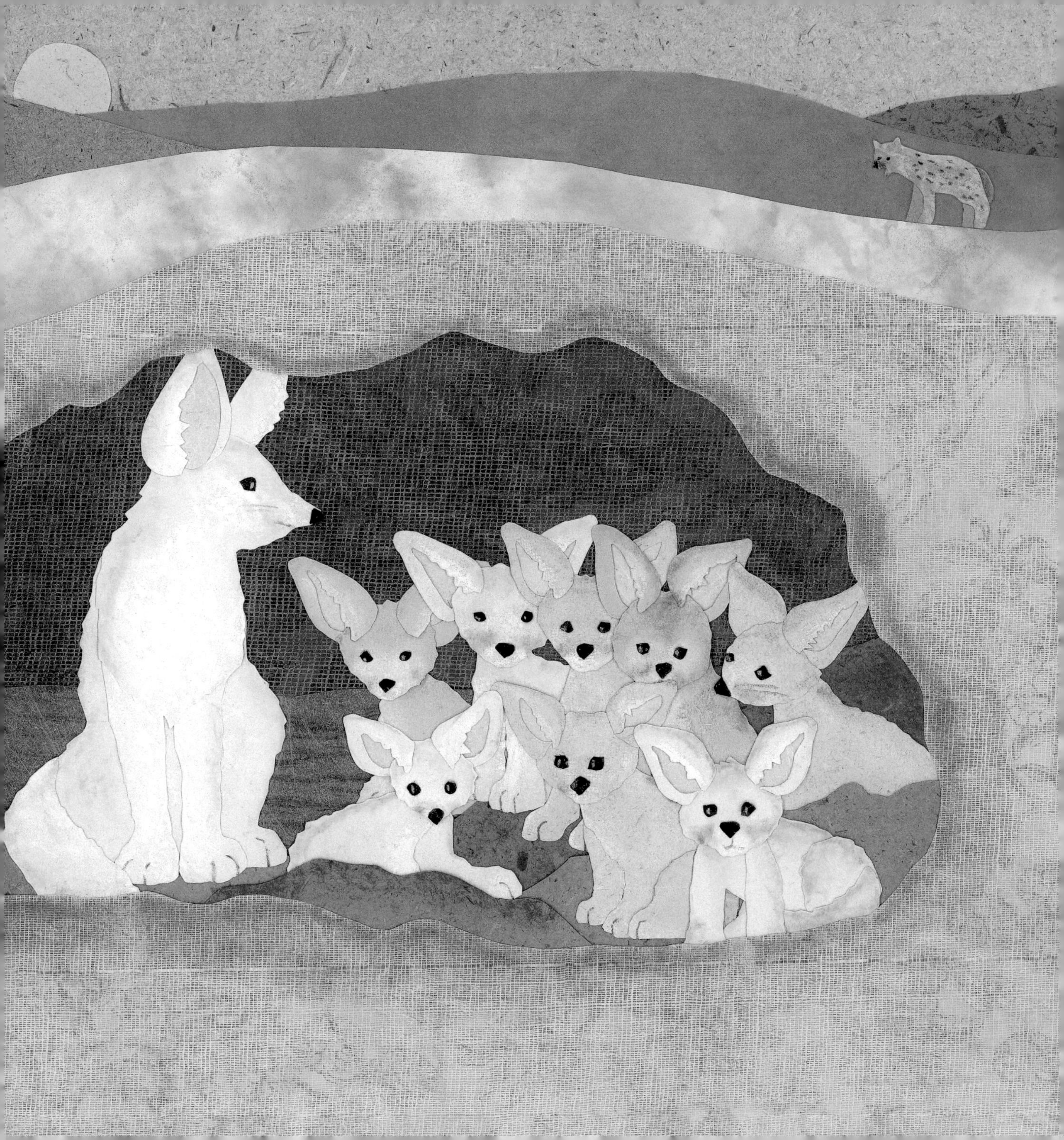

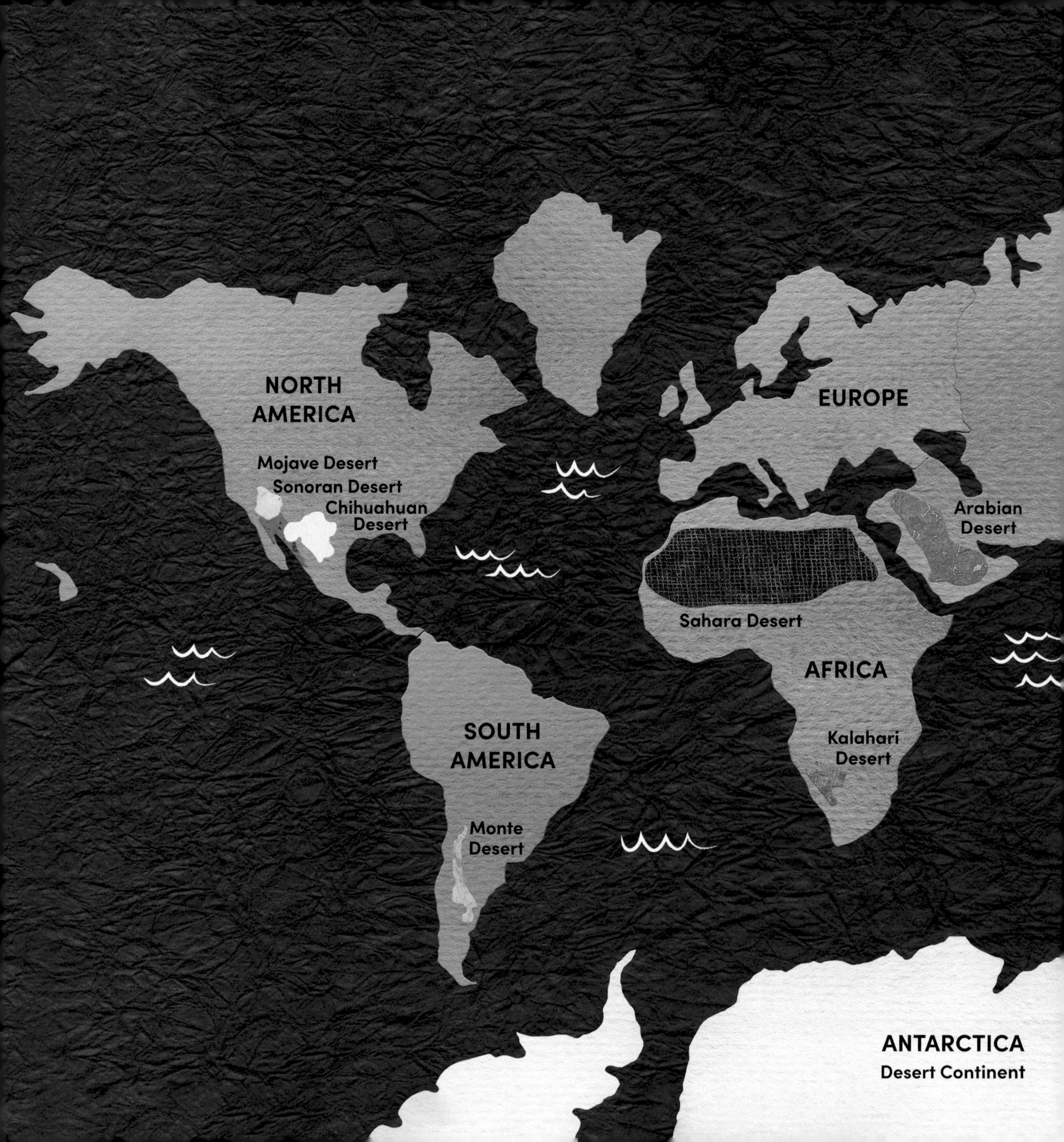
NORTH AMERICA
Mojave Desert
Sonoran Desert
Chihuahuan Desert
EUROPE
Arabian Desert
Sahara Desert
AFRICA
Kalahari Desert
SOUTH AMERICA
Monte Desert
ANTARCTICA
Desert Continent

ASIA

Gobi Desert

Great Sandy Desert

AUSTRALIA

Around the world are deserts.
Some are very far away.
Can you find the different deserts
where the baby animals play?

Then go back to the beginning
and spy with your eyes
to find the hidden creatures.
Every page has a surprise!

10 fennec foxes
9 roadrunners
8 jerboas
7 desert tortoises
6 javelina
5 armadillos
4 dingoes
3 meerkats
2 gila monsters
1 camel

## Fact or Fiction?

In this variation of the song "Over in the Meadow," all the desert animals actually behave as they have been portrayed. Camels kneel, armadillos dig, and roadrunners coo. That's a fact! But do they have the number of babies as in this rhyme? No! That is fiction. Gila monsters lay three to fourteen eggs, not two as in this story, and dingoes can have a litter of as many as ten pups. But the author created her story to rhyme, so she combined fact and fiction.

Baby animals are cared for in different ways by their parents. Usually, it is the mother who takes care of the babies. But both mother and father roadrunners take care of their chicks until they are no longer helpless. And a father fennec fox hunts for food for his kits. However, male javelina take no part in raising or protecting their babies. Nature has different ways of ensuring the survival of different species.

## Desert Facts

About 20 percent of all land on Earth is desert. Deserts are defined by the amount of precipitation they receive, but dry doesn't always mean hot. Did you know there about both hot *and* cold deserts? All of the deserts in this book are hot deserts with the exception of the Gobi, a cold desert in Asia. The largest desert on Earth is completely covered in ice—Antarctica, the polar desert continent.

Deserts receive less than 10 inches (24 mm) of moisture a year. Scientist believe that there are some areas of Antarctica that have not received any precipitation in fourteen million years! Plants that live in this extremely dry habitat have adaptations to help them survive. For example, the shallow root system of a saguaro cactus spreads out near the surface of the desert to collect as much water as possible after a rain. And its thick stem stores water for times of drought. The spines on a barrel cactus not only keep animals from eating it, they also prevent water loss by reflecting away sunlight. Wildflower seeds can remain dormant for dozens of years. When there is a wet season, they burst into vibrant blooms.

One of the ways animals have adapted to living in the desert is by minimizing the time they spend in the hot sun. They're nocturnal (active at night) and crepuscular (active at dawn and dusk). Some animals rest in whatever shade they can find during the day, such as under a camelthorn tree on the Kalahari Desert. Other animals dig below the soil to escape intense heat. Some rodents even plug the entrances to their burrows to keep out the hot air. Staying out of the heat helps animals conserve the water they get from the plants or animals they eat.

## The "Hidden" Animals

**Desert hedgehogs**, found in Africa and the Middle East, escape the heat by staying in their burrows by day and hunting by night. One of the smallest species of hedgehog, they eat a varied diet, including insects, bird eggs, snakes, and scorpions.

**Gambel's quail** are ground-dwelling birds that live in the Sonoran, Mohave, and Chihuahuan Deserts. They prefer to walk or run rather than fly, but when frightened they burst into sudden, short flights. They live in large groups called "coveys," scratching for food under shrubs and cacti.

**Gerbils** are native to sandy areas of Africa, the Middle East, and Asia. They are nocturnal, taking advantage of cooler nights to search for food, which they often bring back to their burrows.

**Blue-tongued skinks** are lizards that bask in the hot Australian sun. When threatened, they stick out their large, blue tongues to scare away predators, and if caught, they bite off their own tails to escape! Their tails will eventually grow back.

**Tarantulas** are large, hairy spiders that live in warm areas around the world. South America has the greatest concentration. They live in underground burrows during the day, killing their prey at night with their venomous fangs. Despite their size, tarantulas are harmless to humans!

**Harris hawks** soar in groups high overhead in the Sonoran Desert to spot animals on the ground. Known as "wolves of the air," they use a cooperative hunting strategy—two or more hawks flush an animal from cover so that it may be captured by another hawk. Prey includes rabbits, ground squirrels, and rodents.

**Elf owls** are the world's smallest owl, about the size of a soda can. Abandoned woodpecker holes made in saguaro cacti in the Sonoran Desert provide safe places for elf owls to nest and raise their young. At night these tiny birds prey on arthropods, such as crickets, moths, and even scorpions.

**Central Asian pit vipers** are venomous snakes that hunt primarily at night, feeding on rodents, lizards, frogs, and insects. They open their mouths wide (180 degrees) to inject venom into their prey

**Painted lady butterflies** spend the winter in the Sonoran Desert from November to early May. After a cool night in the desert, they warm up in the morning sun before flying off to sip nectar from flowers. They migrate north for the summer.

**Spotted hyenas** can be found along the southern edge of the Sahara Desert and adjacent savannas. These carnivores are sometimes solitary scavengers, but will also hunt in packs for prey. The sound of their laughter is one of the most recognizable sounds of Africa.

## About the Animals

**Camels** have pads of thick, leathery skin on their leg joints enabling them to kneel in the hot sand. There are two types of camels: the dromedary, with one hump, and the Bactrian, with two humps. The dromedary, also called the Arabian camel, is the one in this book. Well-adapted to desert life, camels have three sets of eyelids to keep out sand: two with eyelashes and a third clear eyelid to protect their eyes from sandstorms. Camels can go without water for about a week and without food for several months. Their humps store fat, not water, and they also absorb heat. Camels usually have one baby called a calf.

**Gila monsters** (pronounced HEE-luh) are one of the few poisonous lizards in the world. Native to the United States, they spend most of the day under cover or in burrows. Hunting at night, they flick their forked tongues to sense their prey (small mammals, birds, frogs, and other lizards) which they swallow whole. Because they store fat in their tails, they can go without food for months. A female lays an average of five eggs, then leaves the nest! About four months later, the hatchlings emerge and must survive on their own.

**Meerkats** are small mammals about the size of a squirrel. They dig underground burrows in the Kalahari Desert, where they live in small groups called mobs. They often use their long tails as a third leg to stand upright as they keep watch for predators. One meerkat acts as a lookout, while the mob searches for food. If a predator is spotted, the guard lets out a shrill cry, letting group know to run for safety. Meerkats are primarily insectivores, but they will also eat lizards and snakes. They can even eat scorpions because they're immune to the scorpion's strong venom. They produce two to four pups a year.

**Dingoes** are medium-sized wild dogs that live primarily in Australia, but are able to survive in a variety of habitats, and are also found in Southeast Asia. Unlike most dogs, they do not bark, but they sometimes howl like wolves. They're social animals that live in packs of about ten animals. Hunting at night, either alone or in a group, dingoes use their keen sense of smell to sniff for prey which includes rats, rabbits, birds, lizards, and even kangaroos. They will also eat fruits and plants. Dingoes have one litter of five to six pups a year.

**Screaming hairy armadillos** get their name from the squealing noise they make if they're threatened. Like all armadillos, much of this animal's body is covered with a thick armor, but they have more hair than other types of armadillos. Screaming hairy armadillos are native to the Monte Desert, just east of the Andes Mountains in South America. They like loose soil so they can dig burrows and escape predators. Once a year, two pups are born in a litter. Often one is male and one is female.

**Javelina** (pronounced Hah-vuh-LEE-nuh) is a common name for a type of wild hog also known as a collared peccary because the light hair around their necks can look like a collar. They live in family groups of ten or more in southwestern U.S. deserts, as well as Mexico, Central America, and northern Argentina. They communicate with each other with snorts, squeals, woofs, and by clicking their teeth. Mainly nocturnal herbivores, they eat a variety of plants, including the prickly pear cactus. They typically have two babies, called "reds" because of the color of their hair when young.

**Desert tortoises** have lived in the Sonoran Desert for millions of years. They hide from predators by completely withdrawing their heads and limbs into their shells. Their strong forearms and sharp nails help them dig long burrows where they can escape the heat. They are herbivores, eating primarily wildflowers when in bloom, and also grasses, and cacti. A desert tortoise can go up to a year without drinking water. A female tortoise lays one to fourteen eggs. Unlike the mother in the story, she leaves before the hatchlings come out of their shells, so they must survive on their own.

**Gobi jerboas** (pronounced go-bee jer-BO-uh) are rodents that are adapted to living in the cold Gobi desert. Other species of jerboas are adapted for hot deserts. They always walk on their hind legs, rather than on all fours, using their extremely long tails for balance when running. They are most active at night, using their whiskers to feel their surroundings in the dark. Their huge ears give them excellent hearing. Jerboas can jump 10 feet (3 m) when being chased by a predator. Females have two to six pups in each litter and usually have two to three litters a year.

**Roadrunners** are birds prefer to run rather than fly. While capable of flight, their tiny wings can only keep them airborne for a few seconds at a time, but they can run at speeds of up to 15 miles (24 km) per hour. With two toes facing forward and two backwards, they make X-shaped tracks. Also called ground cuckoos, they make cooing calls to communicate. Roadrunners are omnivores that feed on fruit, lizards, rodents, and insects. They even eat venomous rattlesnakes and scorpions. Females lay "clutches" of three to eight white eggs in cup-like nests in mesquite bushes or cacti where the chicks will hatch.

**Fennec foxes** have enormous ears that help them listen for their prey from a long distance in the Sahara Desert. Their ears also help them stay cool by releasing excess heat. Another way they stay cool is to stay in their underground dens during the day. They hunt at night for small animals, insects, lizards, birds, and eggs. They can survive without access to water, getting whatever they need from their food. They live in groups of as many as ten and mark their territory with urine. A female gives birth to a litter of one to five kits.

## Tips from the Author

### BY THE NUMBERS

As stated in "Fact or Fiction," the number of babies in the rhyme isn't necessarily the actual number of babies each animal has. The actual number of babies is explained in "About the Animals." Compare the number of fictional and factual babies to discover the similarities and differences. For example, the camel in the rhyme has one calf, and camels in the desert usually have just one calf—the number of baby camels is the same. The fennec fox in the rhyme has ten kits, but fennec foxes in the desert have from one to five kits—the number of baby fennec foxes is different. You may use the comparisons to create addition or subtraction problems.

### A CLOSER LOOK AT DESERTS AROUND THE WORLD

Look at the map at the end of the story and ask children to name the continents where deserts are found. Which continent doesn't have a desert? Which desert in the story is a cold desert? Which deserts are in the United States? Have children make a pie graph showing that 20 percent of the land on Earth is desert. Older children can make bar graphs showing the size of each desert.

### DESIGN A DESERT ANIMAL

Ask children to design a desert animal that uses at least one adaptation for living in the desert. Children may make a drawing of their animal, or you may provide various supplies and art materials to have them create a 3-D model. Have children draw or paint a desert mural on butcher paper to serve as a backdrop to display their creations.

### CREATE A CACTI GARDEN

Because cacti come in a variety of shapes and sizes, they make an interesting indoor garden. Different types of cacti may be planted together in a shallow, unglazed terra-cotta pot using a mixture of half coarse sand, half houseplant potting soil. Water the cacti well when first planted. Once their roots are established, be careful not to overwater. The cacti will grow well in a location with a lot of light—a southern or southeastern exposure is ideal.

### FUN WITH WORDS

Create a "word wall" to introduce new vocabulary words from the story, such as thrive, crepuscular, mesquite, cacti, aridity, drought, and evaporation. After reading the story, have children add other words to the wall that relate to a desert or animal. Children can use the words in a creative writing activity or in captions to pictures they draw.

## Tips from the Illustrator

Each page of a book is unique. Every illustration must stand on its own, and it also needs to fit into the book as a whole. The author often gives me some indication as to what should be included in my illustration. In *Over on a Desert*, each animal is doing something. The dingo is sniffing, the armadillo is digging, and the jerboa is jumping. Along with the action of each animal, many of these animals are active at a specific time of day. The story says that the jerboas "often go out late," which told me I'd be drawing a night scene. It's always a challenge to draw a nighttime illustration because I want it to be obvious that it's dark out, yet it can't be so dark that you can't see the animals clearly.

I have lots of papers that I use for my illustrations, but I often find I'm looking for something just a little different from what's in front of me. So I experiment to see how I can get what I want. For the jerboa, I used pastels to mute the papers to create a night scene.

Fennec foxes are also active at night, and I decided to create a scene at sunset. The kits are inside their den listening to the coming night sounds from the world outside. Because it's sunset, I could use warm colors that show night approaching, but it's not completely dark like the sky on the jerboa illustration. I think sunset works well as an ending of the day and also the ending of the book.

# Over on a Desert

Sung to the tune
"Over in the Meadow"

Traditional tune
Words by Marianne Berkes

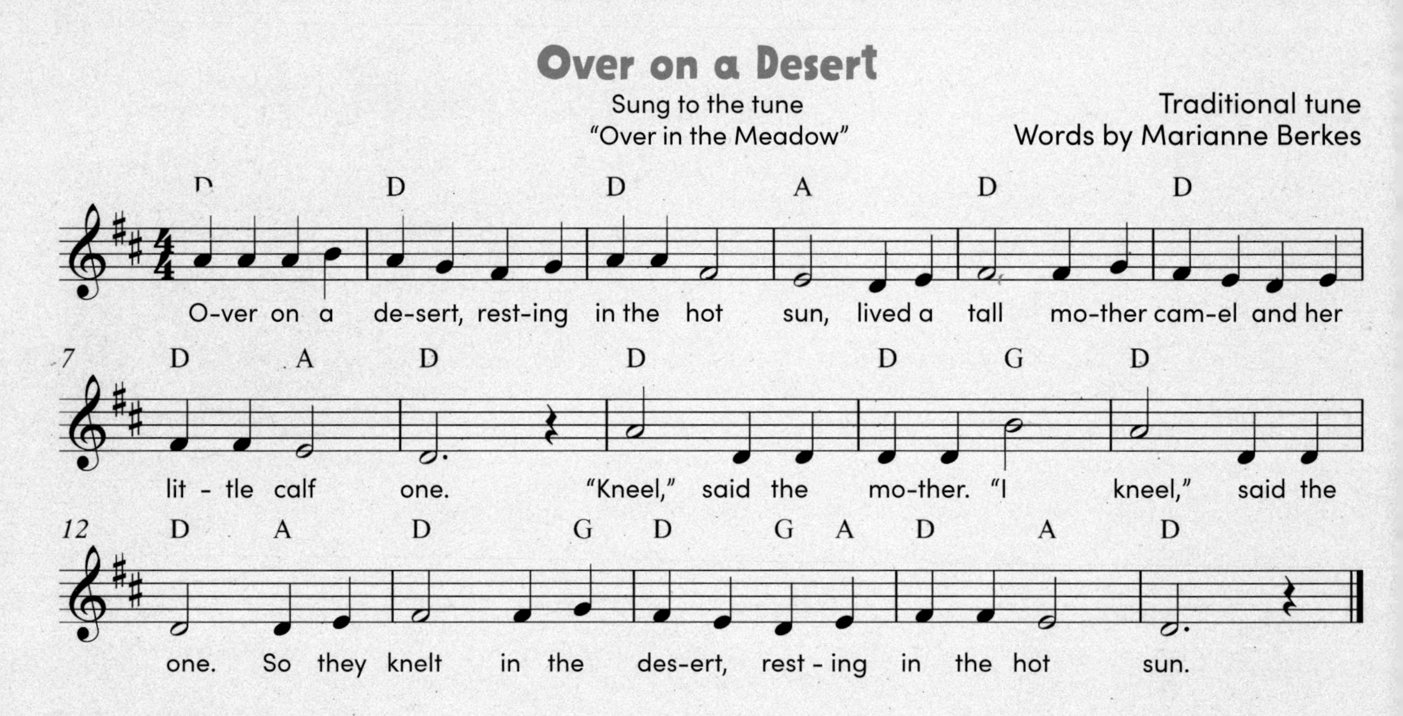

O-ver on a de-sert, rest-ing in the hot sun, lived a tall mo-ther cam-el and her
lit - tle calf one. "Kneel," said the mo-ther. "I kneel," said the
one. So they knelt in the des-ert, rest - ing in the hot sun.

2. Over on a desert, where the barrel cactus grew,
lived a mother gila monster and her little hatchlings two.
"Flick," said the mother. "We flick," said the two.
So they flicked with their tongues, where the barrel cactus grew.

3. Over on a desert, near a camelthorn tree,
lived a slender mother meerkat and her little pups three.
"Stand" said the mother "We stand," said the three.
So they stood and they watched near a camelthorn tree.

4. Over on a desert, on a hot, sandy floor,
lived a wild mother dingo and her little pups four.
"Sniff," said the mother. "We sniff," said the four.
So they sniffed in a pack on a hot, sandy floor.

5. Over on a desert, where mesquite trees thrive,
lived a mother armadillo and her little pups five.
"Dig," said the mother. "We dig," said the five.
So they dug with their claws where mesquite trees thrive.

6. Over on a desert, eating cactus that pricks,
lived a mother javelina and her little reds six.
"Snort," said the mother. "We snort," said the six.
So they grunted and they snorted, eating cactus that pricks.

7. Over on a desert, where saguaros reach the heavens,
lived a mother desert tortoise and her little hatchlings seven.
"Hide," said the mother. "We hide," said the seven.
So they hid in their shells, where saguaros reach the heavens.

8. Over on a desert, where they often go out late,
lived a shy mother jerboa and her little pups eight.
"Jump," said the mother. "We jump," said the eight.
So they jumped way up high, where they often go out late.

9. Over on a desert, in the hot sunshine,
lived a mother roadrunner and her little chicks nine.
"Coo," said the mother. "We coo," said the nine.
So they cooed as they ran in the hot sunshine.

10. Over on a desert, in their underground den,
lived a clever desert fox and his little kits ten.
"Listen," said the father. "We listen," said the ten,
as they heard the sound of laughing from their underground den.

**Marianne Berkes** has spent much of her life as an early childhood educator, children's theater director, and children's librarian. She is the award-winning author of over twenty-three interactive picture books that make learning fun. Her books, inspired by her love of nature, open kids' eyes to the magic found in our natural world. Marianne hopes young children will want to read each book again and again, each time learning something new and exciting. Her website is MarianneBerkes.com.

**Jill Dubin's** whimsical art has appeared in over thirty children's books. Her cut-paper illustrations reflect her interest in combining color, pattern, and texture. She grew up in Yonkers, New York, and graduated from Pratt Institute. She lives with her family in Cape Cod, including two dogs that do very little but with great enthusiasm. Visit her at JillDubin.com.

**To my friend and editor, Carol Malnor.**
**—MB**

**To Marianne Berkes, your words are an inspiration for me and all who are touched by them.**
**—JD**


Series design by Kelley Lanuto

Sourcebooks, Dawn Publications, and the colophon are registered trademarks of Sourcebooks.



Published by Dawn Publications, an imprint of Sourcebooks eXplore
P.O. Box 4410, Naperville, Illinois 60567-4410
(630) 961-3900
sourcebookskids.com

Originally published in 2018 in the United States by Dawn Publications.

Library of Congress Cataloging-in-Publication Data is on file with the publisher.

Source of Production: Wing King Tong Paper Products Co. Ltd., Shenzhen, Guangdong Province, China
Date of Production: July 2021
Run Number: 5020849

Printed and bound in China.
WKT 10 9 8 7 6 5 4 3 2 1

## ALSO BY MARIANNE BERKES AND DAWN PUBLICATIONS

*Baby on Board: How Animal Parents Carry their Young* — These are some of the clever ways animals carry their babies!

*Over in the Ocean* — With unique and outstanding style, this book portrays a vivid community of marine creatures.

*Over in the Jungle* — As with *Ocean*, this book captures a rain forest teeming with remarkable animals.

*Over in the Arctic* — Another charming counting rhyme introduces creatures of the tundra.

*Over in the Forest* — Follow the tracks of forest animals, but watch out for the skunk!

*Over in Australia* — Australian animals are often unique, many with pouches for the babies. Such fun!

*Over in a River* — Beavers, manatees, and so many more animals help teach the geography and habitats of ten great North American rivers.

*Over on a Mountain* — Twenty cool animals, ten great mountain ranges, and seven continents, all in one story!

*Over in the Grasslands* — Come along on a safari! Lions, rhinos, and hippos introduce the African Savanna.

*Over on the Farm* — Welcome to the farm, where pigs roll, goats nibble, horses gallop, hens peck, and turkeys strut! Count, clap, and sing along.

*Going Around the Sun: Some Planetary Fun* — Earth is part of a fascinating "family" of planets.

*Going Home: The Mystery of Animal Migration* — A book that is an introduction to animals that migrate.

*Seashells by the Seashore* — Kids discover, identify, and count twelve beautiful shells to give Grandma for her birthday.

*The Swamp Where Gator Hides* — Still as a log, only his watchful eyes can be seen.

*What's in the Garden?* — Good food doesn't begin on a store shelf in a box. It comes from a garden bursting with life!

## OTHER NATURE BOOKS FROM DAWN PUBLICATIONS

*Tall Tall Tree* — Take a peek at some of the animals that make their home in a tall, tall tree—a magnificent coast redwood. Rhyming verses and a one-to-ten counting scheme made this a real page-turner.

*Daytime Nighttime, All Through the Year* — Delightful rhymes depict two animals for each month, one active during the day and one busy at night. See all the action!

*Octopus Escapes Again!* — Swim along with Octopus as she searches for food. Will she eat or be eaten? She outwits dangerous enemies by using a dazzling display of defenses.

*Paddle, Perch, Climb: Bird Feet Are Neat* — Become a bird detective as you meet the feet that help birds eat—so many different shapes, sizes, and ways to use them. It's time for lunch!

*Dandelion Seed's Big Dream* — A charming tale that follows a seed as it floats from the countryside to the city and encounters all sorts of obstacles and opportunities.

*A Moon of My Own* — An adventurous young girl journeys around the world accompanied by her faithful companion, the Moon. Wonder and beauty await you.